50

A Christmas Feast

Other Clarion Books by Edna Barth

Holly, Reindeer, and Colored Lights:
The Story of the Christmas Symbols

Balder and the Mistletoe:
A Story for the Winter Holidays

Shamrocks, Harps, and Shillelaghs:
The Story of the St. Patrick's Day Symbols

Hearts, Cupids, and Red Roses:
The Story of the Valentine's Day Symbols

Turkeys, Pilgrims, and Indian Corn:
The Story of the Thanksgiving Symbols

Witches, Pumpkins, and Grinning Ghosts:
The Story of the Halloween Symbols

Lilies, Rabbits, and Painted Eggs:
The Story of the Easter Symbols

Jack O'Lantern: *A Story for Halloween*

Cupid and Psyche: *A Story for Valentine's Day*

I'm Nobody! Who Are You?
The Story of Emily Dickinson

A CHRISTMAS FEAST

Poems, Sayings, Greetings, and Wishes

Compiled by EDNA BARTH
Etchings by Ursula Arndt

Houghton Mifflin/Clarion Books
New York

Printed in the United States of America

Library of Congress Cataloging in Publication Data
Main entry under title: A Christmas feast. "A Clarion book."
Summary: A collection of Christmas poems, carols, and sayings by a variety of authors spanning several centuries.
1. Christmas—Juvenile poetry. 2. Children's poetry. [1. Christmas poetry]
I. Barth, Edna. II. Arndt, Ursula.
PN6110.C5C567 808.81'9'33 79-13282 ISBN 0-395-28965-3

Acknowledgments

For permission to use certain poems in this anthology, grateful acknowledgment is made to the following:

A.S. Barnes & Co., Inc. for four lines from a Galician Spanish carol from *Spanish Fiestas* by Nina Epton.

Christian Herald Association for "Christmas" by Faith Baldwin, copyright © 1949 by Christian Herald Association.

Marchette Chute for "Christmas" from *Around and About* by Marchette Chute. Copyright © 1957 (E. P. Dutton) and reprinted by permission of the author.

Elizabeth Coatsworth for her "Eerily Sweet."

Thomas Y. Crowell for "Christmas Candles" and "Country Christmas" by Aileen Fisher from *Skip Around the Year* by Aileen Fisher. Copyright © 1967 by Aileen Fisher. By permission of Thomas Y. Crowell. And for "Merry Christmas" from *Feathered Ones and Furry* by Aileen Fisher. Copyright © 1971 by Aileen Fisher. By permission of Thomas Y. Crowell. Excerpt from *Every Man Heart Lay Down* by Lorenz Graham. Originally appeared as a portion of *How Good Fix Jonah.* Copyright © 1946, 1974 by Lorenz Graham. By permission of Thomas Y. Crowell.

The Dial Press for "The Tree" and "The Wreath" by Paul Engle, excerpted from the book *An Old Fashioned Christmas* by Paul Engle. Copyright © 1964 by Paul Engle. Reprinted by permission of The Dial Press.

Dodd, Mead & Company for "Christmas Song" by Bliss Carman. Reprinted by permission of Dodd, Mead & Company, Inc. from *Poems* by Bliss Carman; and for "Ring Out Ye Bells" from *The Complete Poems of Paul Laurence Dunbar.* Reprinted by permission of Dodd, Mead & Company, Inc.

Aileen Fisher for her "December" and "When Christmas Comes."

Trustees of the Hardy Estate and the Macmillan Administration (Basingstoke) Ltd. for "The Oxen" from *Collected Poems of Thomas Hardy.*

Harper & Row, Publishers, Inc. for "Winter Solstice Chant" from *Being of the Sun* by Ramon Sender and Alicia Bay Laurel. Copyright © 1973 by Ramon Sender and Alicia Bay Laurel. By permission of Harper & Row, Publishers, Inc.; "Under the Mistletoe" from *Copper Sun* by Countee Cullen. Copyright 1927 by Harper & Row, Publishers, Inc. Copyright 1955 by Ida M. Cullen. By permission of Harper & Row, Publishers, Inc.

The Horn Book, Inc. for "Carol for a New Zealand Child" by Dorothy Neal White. Reprinted from *The Horn Book Magazine* Nov.–Dec. 1947. Copyright 1947 by The Horn Book, Inc.

Indiana University Press for "The Stable" by Gabriela Mistral from *Selected Poems of Gabriela Mistral,* translated by Langston Hughes.

Robert Jackson for "Said Simple Sam" by Leroy F. Jackson.

Bertha Klausner International Literary Agency, Inc. for "Christmas Wish" by Elizabeth Searle Lamb. Reprinted by permission of Bertha Klausner International Literary Agency, Inc.

Alfred A. Knopf, Inc. for "December" by John Updike from *A Child's Calendar* by John Updike. Copyright © 1965 by John Updike and Nancy Burkert. Reprinted by permission of Alfred A. Knopf, Inc.

The Lois Lenski Covey Foundation, Inc. for "Old Santa Is an Active Man" by Lois Lenski from *Skipping Village* by Lois Lenski. Copyright © 1927 by the Lois Lenski Covey Foundation, Inc., renewed 1955.

J. B. Lippincott Company and Harold Ober Associates, Inc. for "The Brown Birds" by Eleanor Farjeon from *Poems for Children* by Eleanor Farjeon, published 1951 by J. B. Lippincott Company, copyright 1927, © renewed 1955 by Eleanor Farjeon, copyright 1951 by Eleanor Farjeon. Reprinted by permission of J. B. Lippincott Company and Harold Ober Associates, Inc.

Clark C. Livensparger for "Winter Night" from *Toward Daybreak* by Collister Hutchison. Copyright 1950 and renewed 1977 by Archibald C. Hutchison.

Macmillan Publishing Co., Inc. for "Twelfth Night" and "Wood's Litany" by Elizabeth Coatsworth. Reprinted with permission of Macmillan Publishing Co., Inc. from *Country Poems* by Elizabeth Coatsworth. Copyright 1931, 1933, 1934, 1935, 1936, 1938, 1942 by Elizabeth Coatsworth, renewed 1959, 1961, 1962, 1963, 1964, 1966, 1970 by Elizabeth Coatsworth Beston; for "City Lights" by Rachel Field. Reprinted with permission of Macmillan Publishing Co., Inc. from *Poems* by Rachel Field. Copyright 1924, 1930 by Macmillan Publishing Co., Inc.; for "Christmas at Freelands" by James Stephens. Reprinted from *Collected Poems* of James Stephens with permission of Macmillan Publishing Co., Inc. and of Mrs. Iris Wise and Macmillan, London, and Basingbroke and Canada.

McGraw-Hill Book Company for "Christmas Eve Legend" by Frances Frost from *The Little Whistler* by Frances Frost, copyright 1949 by McGraw-Hill Book Company.

Harold Ober Associates, Inc. for "Angels Wings" by Langston Hughes from *Selected Poems* by Langston Hughes, published 1959 by Alfred A. Knopf, Inc., reprinted by permission of Harold Ober Associates, Inc., copyright © 1959 by Langston Hughes; "Anonymous Verse" translated by Langston Hughes. Reprinted by permission of

Harold Ober Associates, Inc. Copyright © 1963 by Langston Hughes. "Carol of the Brown King" by Langston Hughes from *Crisis,* published 1958 by Crisis Publishing Co., reprinted by permission of Harold Ober Associates, Inc., copyright © 1958 by Crisis Publishing Co.; and "Shepherd's Song at Christmas" by Langston Hughes from *The Langston Hughes Reader,* published 1958 by George Braziller, Inc., reprinted by permission of Harold Ober Associates, Inc., copyright © 1958 by Langston Hughes.

Plays, Inc., Publishers for "Christmas Tree" by Aileen Fisher © copyright 1960 by Aileen Fisher. Reprinted by permission from *Christmas Plays and Programs* by Aileen Fisher. Plays, Inc., Publishers, Boston, MA.

Rand McNally & Company, publishers for "Duckle, Duckle, Daisy" by Leroy F. Jackson from *The Peter Patter Book* by Leroy F. Jackson. Copyright 1918, renewal copyright 1946 by Rand McNally & Company, publishers.

Laura Mincieli Ross for "Oh, My Bambino".

Routledge & Kegan Paul Ltd for "A Child Is Born" by Mary Ann Hamburger from *Poems by Children* chosen by Michael Baldwin. London: Routledge & Kegan Paul Ltd. © copyright 1962.

Marguerita Rudolph for "Granny Winter" and "Yolka".

Charles Scribner's Sons for "Carol" by Kenneth Grahame from *Wind in the Willows,* reprinted with the permission of Charles Scribner's Sons from *Wind in the Willows* by Kenneth Grahame, copyright 1908 Charles Scribner's Sons, and for "Christmas Eve" by Marion Edey and Dorothy Grider, reprinted from *Open the Door* by Marion Edey and Dorothy Grider with the permission of Charles Scribner's sons, copyright 1949 by Marion Edey and Dorothy Grider.

Isabel Shaw for her "A Christmas Chant," first published in *Jack & Jill,* December 1949.

Melvin Lee Steadman, Jr. for "The Christmas Star" by Nancy Byrd Turner. Permission by Melvin Lee Steadman, Jr.

University of Texas Press for "The Three Kings" by Rubén Darío from *Selected Poems of Rubén Darío,* translated by Lysander Kemp. Copyright © 1965 University of Texas Press. All rights reserved; and for "The Star That Came" and "You Light" by Juan Ramón Jiménez from *Three Hundred Poems by Juan Ramón Jiménez 1903–1953,* translated by Eloise Roach. Copyright © Francisco H.-Pinzon Jiménez. All rights reserved. University of Texas Press 1962.

The Viking Press (Viking Penguin Inc.) for "The Ballad of Befana" by Phyllis McGinley from *Merry Christmas, Happy New Year* by Phyllis McGinley. Copyright © Phyllis McGinley 1958. All rights reserved. Reprinted by permission of Viking Penguin Inc.

Chad Walsh for his "Christmas in the Straw."

Yale University Press for "Bundles" by John Farrar from *Songs for Parents* by John Farrar. Copyright © 1921 by Yale University Press.

Diligent efforts have been made to trace the ownership of all copyrighted material in this volume. If any errors have inadvertently been made, they will be corrected in subsequent editions, provided that the publisher is notified.

To Bill Evans

Contents

Introduction

In exploring the origins of the Christmas holiday for *Holly, Reindeer, and Colored Lights,* my book about the Christmas symbols, I came upon a wealth of poems, rhymes, carols, mottoes, and superstitions, many of which were totally new to me or only dimly remembered. Soon, almost of itself, a collection was underway.

Some of the items are so archaic that the English is like another language. Many are of folk origin and have a refreshing innocence and what Emily Dickinson might have called "a simple majesty." Others are by such masters of English literature as Milton and Shakespeare.

In some of the earlier selections there are traces of pre-Christian worship of solar deities. Visible in even the most modern of Christmas poems are reminders of the winter solstice rites that persisted well into Christian times—the meaning of holiday evergreens, for example, or flaming yule logs, lights, and candles.

Changing attitudes toward Christmas celebrations through the ages are reflected in the output and quality of Christmas poetry, which reached its fullest glory in the sixteenth and early seventeenth centuries. With the Puritan influences of the seventeenth century came a marked decline. The next two hundred years saw many writers turning to Christmas themes, but works of distinction seem to have been the exception rather than the rule. Not until the twentieth century could it be said that Christmas poetry was coming into its own again.

For each new generation of children, Christmas is as filled with magic and wonder as for any previous generation. And what holiday more truly belongs to children than one which hails the birth of a little child? With this in mind, I have drawn from my own collection of Christmas poetry and the lore of some five centuries a sampling I hope children will enjoy.

Christmas Is Coming

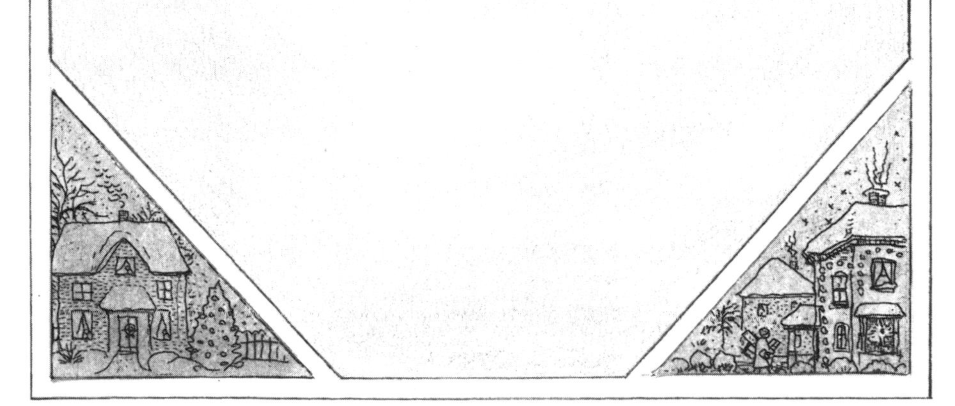

The dark night wakes, the glory breaks,
    And Christmas comes once more.

from "O Little Town of Bethlehem"
by Phillips Brooks, 1835–1893

❦ *The Twenty-fourth of December*

The clock ticks slowly, slowly in the hall,
And slower and more slow the long hours crawl;
It seems as though today
Would never pass away;
The clock ticks slowly, s-l-o-w-l-y in the hall.

Author unknown

Said Simple Sam: "Does Christmas come
    In April or December,
In winter, spring, or harvest time?
    I really can't remember."

Leroy F. Jackson, 20th century

Christmas comes, he comes, he comes,
Ushered in with a rain of plums,
Hollies in the windows greet him,
Schools come driving post to meet him,
Gifts precede him, bells proclaim him,
Every voice delights to name him.

English traditional

Christmas-tide Comes in like a Bride

When Christmas-tide comes in like a bride,
With holly and ivy clad,
Twelve days in the year, much mirth and good
cheer
In every household is had.

from The Praise of Christmas, *1630*

Chill December brings the sleet,
Blazing fire, and Christmas treat.

from The Garden Year
by Sara Coleridge, 20th century

Christmas

Christmas is coming, the geese are
getting fat,
Please to put a penny in an old
man's hat;
If you haven't got a penny, a
ha'penny will do,
If you haven't got a ha'penny,
God bless you.

Mother Goose

Christmas

My goodness, my goodness,
It's Christmas again.
The bells are all ringing.
I do not know when
I've been so excited.
The tree is all fixed,
The candles are lighted,
The pudding is mixed.

The wreath's on the door
And the carols are sung,
The presents are wrapped
And the holly is hung.
The turkey is sitting
All safe in its pan,
And I am behaving
As calm as I can.

Marchette Chute, 20th century

December

I like days
with a snow-white collar,
and nights when the moon
is a silver dollar,
and hills are filled
with eiderdown stuffing
and your breath makes smoke
like an engine puffing.

I like days
when feathers are snowing,
and all the eaves
have petticoats showing,
and the air is cold
and the wires are humming,
But you feel all warm . . .
with Christmas coming.

Aileen Fisher, 20th century

December

First snow! The flakes
  So few, so light,
Remake the world
  In solid white.

All bundled up,
  We feel as if
We were fat penguins,
  Warm and stiff.

Downtown, the stores
  Half split their sides,
And Mother brings home
  Things she hides.

Old carols peal.
  The dusk is dense.
There is a mood
  Of sweet suspense.

The shepherds wait,
  The kings, the tree—
All wait for something
  Yet to be,

Some miracle.
  And then it's here,
Wrapped up in hope—
  Another year!

John Updike, 20th century

Some say that ever again
that season comes wherein
Our Saviour's birth is celebrated
the bird of dawning
singeth all night long.
And then, they say, no spirit
dare stir abroad.
No planet strikes.
No fairy takes nor witch
hath power to charm.
So hallowed and so
gracious is the time.

from Hamlet
by William Shakespeare, 1564–1616

Then Light Ye up Your Candles

Christmas Chant

Candle, candle,
  Burning bright
On our window
  Sill tonight,
Like the shining
  Christmas star
Guiding shepherds
  From afar,
Lead some weary
  Traveler here,
That he may share
  Our Christmas cheer.

Isabel Shaw, 20th century

Christmas Candle

Small hands I lift to You who once were small.
Small gifts I bring to You who, in a stall,
Brought to the world the greatest gift of all
    That winter night.

Small as a cricket's chirp the voice I raise
To join the chorus of enduring praise,
Yet once Your voice was small amid the maze
Of singing might.

Small is the Lighted taper that I bear,
But You will see it in the window there—
And for the sake of children everywhere
Will bless its light.

Rachel Field, 20th century

Christmas Candles

In the evening, in the windows,
red and white the candles glow,
so the Christ Child, if He passes,
will be guided through the snow.
No one knows what route He travels,
no one knows when He is nigh,
but each house that shows a candle
will be blessed if He goes by.

Aileen Fisher, 20th century

❦ *Winter Night*

A tree may be laughter in the spring
Or a promise
Or conceit.

In the summer it may be anything
Lazy and warm with life,
Complete.

In the fall
It is the answer
To a long-forgotten call.

But on a lonely winter night
In still air
When it takes the shape of a candle flame
Springing dark from a hill all white,
It is a dare.

Collister Hutchison, 20th century

Then be ye glad, good people,
This night of all the year,
And light ye up your candles:
His star is shining near.

Traditional

At Christmas Time We Deck the Hall

But give me holly, bold and jolly,
Honest, prickly, shining holly;
Pluck me holly leaf and berry
For the days when I make merry.

Christina Georgina Rossetti, 1830–1894

The Holly and the Ivy

The holly and the ivy
    Now both are full well grown.
Of all the trees are in the wood,
    The holly bears the crown.

Traditional

Be links no longer broken;
Be sweet forgiveness spoken,
Under the Holly Bough.

Charles Mackay, 19th century

❧ *Green Grow'th the Holly*

Green grow'th the holly
So doth the ivy;
  Though winter blasts blow ne'er so high,
Green grow'th the holly.

Green grow'th the holly,
So doth the ivy;
  The God of life can never die,
Hope! saith the holly.

English, 16th century

The Mistletoe

It was after the maze and mirth of the dance,
  Where a spray of green mistletoe swayed,
That I met—and I vow that the meeting was
    chance!—
  With a very adorable maid.

I stood for a moment in tremor of doubt,
  Then kissed her, half looking for war:
But—"Why did you wait, Sir!" she said, with a
    pout,
  "Pray, what is the mistletoe for?"

Clinton Scollard, 1860–1932

Under the Mistletoe

I did not know she'd take it so,
  Or else I'd never dared:
Although the bliss was worth the blow,
I did not know she'd take it so.
She stood beneath the mistletoe
So long I thought she cared;
I did not know she'd take it so,
Or else I'd never dared.

Countee Cullen, 20th century

❧ *At Christmas Time*

At Christmas time we deck the hall
  With holly branches brave and tall,
With sturdy pine and hemlock bright
And in the Yule log's dancing light
We tell old tales of field and fight
    At Christmas time.

At Christmas time we pile the board
  With flesh and fruit and vintage stored,
And mid the laughter and the glow
We tread a measure soft and slow,
And kiss beneath the mistletoe
    At Christmas time.

English traditional

❦ *Ever Green*

Each house is swept the day before,
    And windows stuck with evergreens,
The snow is besom'd from the door,
    And comfort crowns the cottage scenes.
Gilt holly, with its thorny pricks
    And yew and box, with berries small,
These deck the unused candlesticks,
    And pictures hanging by the wall.

John Clare, 1793–1864

❦ *The Wreath*

Now Christmas comes
Leafy and floral,
Poinsettia, pine,
The mountain laurel.

Now wreaths of fir,
Of spruce or pine
Hang on the door
With a green shine.

Even the sun,
On earth beneath,
Turns in space
Like a gold wreath.

And men who give
Love and good will,
Are a live wreath
On town and hill.

Paul Engle, 20th century

A Thousand Bells Ring Out

Ring out, ye bells!
All Nature swells
With gladness of the wondrous story,
The world was lorn,
But Christ is born
To change our sadness into glory.

Paul Lawrence Dunbar, 1872–1906

Voices in the Mist

The time draws near the birth of Christ:
The moon is hid; the night is still;
The Christmas bells from hill to hill
Answer each other in the mist.

Four voices of four hamlets round,
From far and near, on mead and moor,
Swell out and fail, as if a door
Were shut between me and the sound:

Each voice four changes on the wind,
That now dilate, and now decrease,
Peace and goodwill, goodwill and peace,
Peace and goodwill, to all mankind.

Alfred, Lord Tennyson, 1809–1892

❦ *A Thousand Bells*

It is the calm and solemn night!
A thousand bells ring out and throw
Their joyous peals abroad, and smile
The darkness, charm'd and holy now!
The night that erst no name had worn,
To it a happy name is given
For in that stable lay new-born
The peaceful Prince of Earth and Heaven,
In the solemn midnight
Centuries ago.

Alfred Domett, 1811–1887

❦ *Christmas Bells*

The singing waits, a merry throng,
    At early morn with simple skill,
Yet imitate the angel's song,
    And chant their Christmas ditty still;
And, mid the storm that dies and swells
    By fits, in hummings softly steals
The music of the village bells,
    Ringing round their merry peals.

John Clare, 1793–1864

Song

Why do bells for Christmas sing?
Why do little children sing?

Once a lovely shining star,
Seen by shepherds from afar,
Gently moved until its light
Made a manger's cradle bright.

There a darling baby lay,
Pillowed soft upon the hay;
And its mother sang and smiled,
"This is Christ, the holy child!"

Therefore bells for Christmas ring,
Therefore little children sing.

Eugene Field, 1850–1895

❦ *Christmas Bells*

I heard the bells on Christmas Day
Their old, familiar carols play.
    And wild and sweet
    The words repeat
Of peace on earth, good-will to men!

And thought how, as the day had come,
The belfries of all Christendom
    Had rolled along
    The unbroken song
Of peace on earth, good-will to men!

Till, ringing, singing on its way,
The world revolved from night to day,
    A voice, a chime,
    A chant sublime
Of peace on earth, good-will to men!

Then from each black, accursed mouth
The cannon thundered in the South,
    And with the sound
    The carols drowned
Of peace on earth, good-will to men!

It was as if an earthquake rent
The hearth-stones of a continent,
    And made forlorn
    The households born
Of peace on earth, good-will to men!

And in despair I bowed my head;
"There is no peace on earth," I said,
    "For hate is strong,
    And mocks the song
Of peace on earth, good-will to men!

Then pealed the bells more loud and deep;
"God is not dead, nor doth He sleep!
    The Wrong shall fail,
    The Right prevail,
With peace on earth, good-will to men!"

Henry Wadsworth Longfellow, 1807–1882

Bells

Oh, he did whistle and she did sing,
And all the bells on earth did ring,
For joy that our Savior He was born
On Christmas Day in the morning.

from an old English carol

Peace on Earth

❦ *The Angels*

And suddenly there was with the angel a multitude of the heavenly host praising God, and saying,
"Glory to God in the highest, and on earth peace, good will toward men."

Luke II:13–14

❦ *And All the Angels*

And all the angels in heaven shall sing,
    On Christmas Day, on Christmas Day,
And all the angels in heaven shall sing,
    On Christmas Day in the morning.

from an old Scottish carol

❦ *Christ Is Born*

Angels clap hands; let men forbear to mourn;
Their saving health is come; for Christ is born.
Hark, what a heavenly choir of angels sing
Sweet carols at the birth of this new king.

English, 16th century (with modern spelling)

❦ *Angels Wings*

The angels wings is white as snow,
O, white as snow,
White
as
Snow.

The angels wings is white as snow,
But I drug ma wings
In the dirty mire.
O, I drug ma wings
All through the fire.
But the angels wings is white as snow,
White
as
snow.

Langston Hughes, 20th century

His place of birth a solemn angel tells
To simple shepherds keeping watch by night;
They gladly thither haste, and by a quire
Of squadroned angels hear his carol sung.

from Paradise Lost *by John Milton,*
1608–1674

And they who do their souls no wrong,
But keep, at eve, the faith of morn,
Shall daily hear the angel-song,
"Today the Prince of Peace is born."

James Russell Lowell, 1819–1891

❦ *Christmas Eve*

On a winter night
When the moon is low
The rabbits hop on the frozen snow.
The woodpecker sleeps in his hole
        in the tree
And fast asleep is the chickadee.
Twelve o'clock
And the world is still
As the Christmas star comes
        over the hill
The angels sing, and sing again:
"Peace on earth, goodwill to men."

Marion Edey and Dorothy Grider, 20th century

Rise, Shepherds

❦ *The Shepherds*

And there were in the same country shepherds abiding in the field, keeping watch over their flock by night

And, lo, the angel of the Lord came upon them, and the glory of the Lord shone round about them: and they were sore afraid.

And the angel said unto them, Fear not: for, behold, I bring you good tidings of great joy, which shall be to all people.

For unto you is born this day in the city of David a Saviour, which is Christ the Lord.

And this shall be *a sign unto you; Ye shall find the babe wrapped in swaddling clothes, lying in a manger.*

Luke II:8–12

❦ *Shepherd's Song at Christmas*

Look there at the star!
I, among the least,
Will arise and take
A journey to the East.
But what shall I bring
As a present for the King?
What shall I bring to the Manger?

> I will bring a song,
> A song that I will sing,
> In the Manger.

Watch out for my flocks,
Do not let them stray.
I am going on a journey
Far, far away.
But what shall I bring
As a present for the Child?
What shall I bring to the Manger?

> I will bring a lamb,
> Gentle, meek, and mild,
> A lamb for the Child
> In the Manger.

Langston Hughes, 20th century

About the Field

About the field they piped full right,
Even about the midst of the night;
They saw come down from heaven a light:
Tirlè, tirlè—so merrily
The shepherds began to blow.

English shepherd's carol

Rise, Shepherds

Rise, shepherds, though the night is deep,
Rise from your slumber's dreaming!
Jesus, the shepherd, watch does keep,
In love all men redeeming.
Hasten to Mary, and look for her Child,
Come, shepherds, and greet our Savior mild!

Austrian shepherd's song

Bring Your Pipes

Bring your pipes and bring your drum,
  Call the shepherds all to come;
Hasten quick, no time to lose,
  Don't forget your dancing shoes.
Frolic we right merrily:
  He will laugh with happy glee,
Yes, and smile, and we will dance,
  While He claps His tiny hands.

Austrian shepherd's song

So Come We Running

So come we running to the crib,
    I and also you,
A bee line into Bethlehem,
    Hopsa, trala, loo!
Oh, baby dear, take anything
    Of all the little gifts we bring,
Take apples or take butter,
    Oh, have some pears or yellow cheese,
Have nuts or plums or what you please.

Austrian shepherd's song

How simple we must grow!
How simple they who came!
The shepherds looked at God
Long before any man.
He sees God nevermore
Not there, nor here on earth
Who does not long within
To be a shepherd first.

from Paradox *by Angelus Silesius, 1624–1677*

❧ *The Shepherds Knew*

The shepherds knew
That the Child wanted a fiesta
And every one of them wore out
A hundred pairs of castanets.

from a Spanish carol

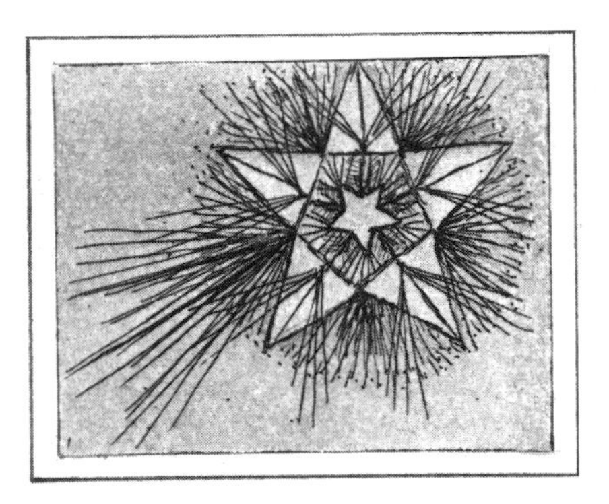

We Have Seen His Star

For we have seen his star in the east, and are come to worship him.

Matthew II:2

There is one glory of the sun, and another glory of the moon, and another glory of the stars: for the one *star differeth from* another *star in glory.*

1st. Corinthians XV

❦ *We Saw a Light*

We saw a light shine out afar
On Christmas in the morning,
And knew we straight it was Christ's star
Bright beaming in the morning.
Then did we fall on bended knee
On Christmas in the morning,
And praised the Lord who'd let us see
His glory at its dawning.

Old English carol

Christmas

The snow is full of silver light
Spilled from the heavens' tilted cup
And, on this holy, tranquil night,
The eyes of men are lifted up
To see the promise written fair,
The hope of peace for all on earth,
And hear the singing bells declare
The marvel of the dear Christ's birth.
The way from year to year is long
And though the road be dark so far,
Bright is the manger, sweet the song,
The steeple rises to the Star.

Faith Baldwin, 20th century

The Star That Came

In the orange tree is the star.
See who can lay hands on it!

Hurry, come with the pearls,
and bring out the nets of silk!

Upon the roof sits the star.
See who can lay hands on it!

Oh, what fragrance of spring
its poem of eternal light!

The star is in someone's eyes.
See who can lay hands on it!

Through the air, in the grass,
take care, it may get lost!

Harbored in love is the star!
See who can lay hands on it!

Juan Ramón Jiménez, 1881–1958

Morning Star

Morning Star, O cheering sight!
Ere thou cam'st, how dark the night!
    Jesus mine, in me shine,
    Fill my heart with light divine.

from a Moravian hymn

One Glorious Star

When Christ was born in Bethlehem
T'was night, but seemed the noon of day.
The stars whose light was pure and bright
Shone with unwavering ray.
But one, one glorious star
Guided the Eastern Magi from afar.

from a Sicilian shepherd's carol,
translated by Henry Wadsworth Longfellow,
1807–1882

And in a far country
God hear a wise man call Him name
And God say to the wise man
    "I send My son to be a new wise man,
    Go now with the star."
And the star call
And the wise man follow.

from Every Man Heart Lay Down
by Lorenz Graham, 20th century

The Christmas Star

High in the heavens a single star,
    of pure, imperishable light;
Out on the desert strange and far
    Dim riders riding through the night:
Above a hilltop sudden song
    Like silver trumpets down the sky—
And all to welcome One so young
    He scarce could lift a cry!

Nancy Byrd Turner, 20th century

A Child Is Born

❦ *The Nativity*

And Joseph also went up from Galilee, out of the city of Nazareth, into Judaea, unto the city of David, which is called Bethlehem (because he was of the house and lineage of David): to be taxed with Mary his espoused wife, being great with child. And so it was, that, while they were there, the days were accomplished that she should be delivered. And she brought forth her firstborn son, and wrapped him in swaddling clothes, and laid him in a manger; because there was no room for them in the inn.

Luke II:1–7

Bethlehem

A little child,
    A shining star,
A stable rude,
    The door ajar,
Yet in this place,
    So crude, forlorn,
The Hope of all
    The world was born.

Author unknown

Carol

I saw a sweet, a seemly sight,
A blissful bird, a blossom bright,
That morning made and mirth among:
A maiden mother meek and mild
In cradle keep a simple child
That softly slept; she sat and sang:
    "Lullay, lulla, balow,
    My babe, sleep softly now."

English, 15th century

The darling of the world is come
And fit it is, we find a roome
To Welcome Him. The nobler part
Of all the house is here, is the heart,
Which we shall give Him; and bequeath this
Hollie,
And this Ivie wreath
To do him honour: who's our king
And Lord of all this reveling.

Robert Herrick, 1591–1674

❦ *Carol for a New Zealand Child*

Christmas in the picture book
Gold and white with snow,
Winter in the desert
Where the three Kings go.
Ice on the camel-rein,
Rime on the crown,
Snow round the stable doors
Of Bethlehem town.

I carol Baby Jesus
On a nor-west day,
A summer wind is blowing
Across the beach and bay.
Sea gulls whirl where
Children run to swim,
Laughter in the breakers
Their Christmas hymn.

Dorothy Neal White, 20th century

Christmas Day

Last night in the open shippen
  The Infant Jesus lay,
While cows stood at the hay-crib
  Twitching the sweet hay.

As I trudged through the snow-fields
  That lay in their own light,
A thorn-bush with its shadow
  Stood doubled on the night.

And I stayed on my journey
  To listen to the cheep
Of a small bird in the thorn-bush
  I woke from its puffed sleep.

The bright stars were my angels
  And with the heavenly host
I sang praises to the Father,
  The Son and Holy Ghost.

Andrew Young, 1807–1889

In Bethlehem is born the Holy Child,
On hay and straw in the winter wild;
O, my heart is full of mirth
At Jesus' birth.

from the Messiah *by*
George Frideric Handel, 1685–1759

A Christmas Carol

Before the paling of the stars,
Before the winter morn,
Before the earliest cock-crow
Jesus Christ was born:
Born in a stable,
Cradled in a manger,
In the world His hands had made
Born a stranger.

Priest and king lay fast asleep
In Jerusalem,
Young and old lay fast asleep
In crowded Bethlehem:
Saint and angel, ox and ass,
Kept a watch together,
Before the Christmas daybreak
In the winter weather.

Jesus on His mother's breast
In the stable cold,
Spotless Lamb of God was He,
Shepherd of the fold:
Let us kneel with Mary maid,
With Joseph bent and hoary,
With saint and angel, ox and ass,
To hail the King of Glory.

Christina Georgina Rossetti, 1830–1894

As Joseph Was A-Walking

As Joseph was a-walking
He heard an angel sing,
"This night shall be the birth-time
Of Christ, the Heavenly King.

He neither shall be born
In house nor in hall,
Nor in a place of paradise,
But in an ox's stall.

He shall not be clothèd
In purple nor in pall;
But in the fair white linen,
That usen babies all.

He neither shall be rockéd
  In silver nor in gold,
But in a wooden manger
  That resteth on the mold."

As Joseph was a-walking
  There did an angel sing,
And Mary's child at midnight
  Was born to be our King.

Then be ye glad, good people,
  This night of all the year,
And light ye up your candles,
  For His star it shineth clear.

Old English

❧ *Christmas at Freelands*

A snowy field! A stable piled
With straw! A donkey's sleepy pow!
A mother beaming on a child!
A manger, and a munching cow!
—These we all remember now—
And airy voices, heard afar!
And three Magicians, and a Star!

Two thousand times of snow declare
That on the Christmas of the year
There is a singing in the air;
And all who listen for it hear
A fairy chime, a seraph strain,
Telling He is born again,
—That all we love is born again.

James Stephens, 1882–1950

A Hymn on the Nativity of My Saviour

I sing the birth was born tonight,
The author both of life and light;
    The angels so did sound it.
And like the ravished shepherds said,
Who saw the light and were afraid,
    Yet searched, and true they found it.

Ben Jonson, 1573–1637

Oh, My Bambino

Thou descended from the stars,
Oh, my Bambino.
Here I see you now,
Here a-trembling.
Do not tremble so
For here is your mother.

from an old Italian carol,
translated by Laura Mincieli Ross,
20th century

Little Jesus of the crib
Give us the virtues of those that surround you
Make us philosophical as the fisherman
Carefree as the drummer
Merry in exploring the world as the troubadour
Eager for work as the bugler
Patient as the spinner
Kind as the ass
Strong as the ox that keeps you warm.

an old French prayer from Provence

❦ *The Stable*

When midnight came
and the Child's cry arose,
a hundred beasts awakened
and the stable became alive.

And drawing near they came
reaching out toward the Child
a hundred eager necks
like a forest swaying.

An ox whose eyes were tender
as though filled with dew,
lowered its head to breathe
quietly in His face.

Against Him rubbed a lamb
with the softest of soft fleece,
and two baby goats squatted,
licking His hands.

The walls of the stable
unnoticed were covered
with pheasants and with geese
and cocks and with blackbirds.

The pheasants flew down
and swept over the Child
tails of many colors;
while the geese with wide bills
smoothed His pallet of straw;
and a swarm of blackbirds
became a veil rising and falling
above the new born.

The Virgin confused among such horns
and whiteness of breathing,
fluttered hither and yon
unable to pick up her Child.

Joseph arrived laughing
to help her in her confusion,
and the upset stable was like
a forest in the wind.

Gabriela Mistral, 20th century,
translated from the Spanish
by Langston Hughes

A Child Is Born

A baby is born, rejoice
How quiet not a noise
Born in a manger
To save us from danger
He was to teach
Love and preach.
Angels sang
As the sheep bells rang.
Shepherds were curious
Herod was furious.
So now keep Christmas day
Lovely, joyous and gay.

by Mary Ann Hamburger, age 8

Long, Long Ago

Winds through the olive trees
    Softly did blow,
Round little Bethlehem
    Long, long ago.

Sheep on the hillside lay
    Whiter than snow
Shepherds were watching them,
    Long, long ago.

Then from the happy sky,
    Angels bent low
Singing their songs of joy,
    Long, long ago.

For in a manger bed,
    Cradled we know,
Christ came to Bethlehem,
    Long, long ago.

Author unknown

Christmas in the Straw

In heaven it's Allemande Left and Promenade
And Swing That Corner Lady One and All.
This is the music that the fiddler played
When stars danced out of nothing at his call.

This is the dance the fiddler danced when Eve
Pranced to her feet from Adam's wounded side.
This is the song the fiddler sang at eve
Beside a cradle and his Jewish bride.

The angels sang the song the fiddler played.
The sheep and shepherds danced a Texas Star,
And wise men heard the music and obeyed;
The camels' feet kept rhythm with a star.

One and all, come this way.
Hear the fiddler sing and play.
Join your hands and form a ring,
Stamp your feet, dance and sing,
Hallelujah, now sashay!

Chad Walsh, 20th century

Though He be Lord of all,
The Christ Child is but very small.
Kneel then, and at His cradle lay,
Most gentle love this Christmas Day.

Anonymous, 14th Century

The Friendly Beasts

The wolf also shall dwell with the lamb,
And the leopard shall lie down with the kid;
And the calf and young lion together;
And a little child shall lead them.

Isaiah II

Christmas Eve Legend

The woods were still and the snow was deep,
But there was no creature who could sleep.

The fox and the vixen ran together
Silently through the starry weather.

The buck and the doe and the fawn came
drifting
Into the clearing. The rabbit, lifting

His ears, shook white from the twigs he
brushed;
The chattering squirrel for once was hushed

As he sat with his paws against his breast,
And the bobcat crouched on the mountain crest.

Safe in the fold the silver sheep
Told the young lambs not to leap.

In the shadowy stable the horses stood
Hearing the quietness in the wood,

And the cattle sighed in the fragrant barn,
Waiting the instant of the morn.

The stars stood at midnight, and tame or wild,
All creatures knelt to worship the Child.

Frances Frost, 20th century

❧ *When Christmas Comes*

Take up the nets from lake and sea!
When Christmas comes let fish swim free.

Take up the traps and wily snares!
Let them have peace the hunted hares.

Let all the creatures sport and play
in peace and trust on Christmas Day,

In honor of the humble Child
Who loved them all, the tame and wild.

Aileen Fisher, 20th century

❦ *The Oxen*

Christmas Eve, and twelve of the clock,
  "Now they are all on their knees,"
An elder said as we sat in a flock
  By the embers in hearthside ease.

We pictured the meek mild creatures where
  They dwelt in their strawy pen,
Nor did it occur to one of us there
  To doubt they were kneeling then.

So fair a fancy few would weave
  In these years! Yet, I feel,
If someone said on Christmas Eve,
  "Come; see the oxen kneel,

"In the lonely barton by yonder coomb
  Our childhood used to know,"
I should go with him in the gloom,
  Hoping it might be so.

Thomas Hardy, 1840–1920

❦ *Twelfth Night*
(The Song of the Camels)

Not born to the forest are we,
Not born to the plain,
To the grass and the shadowed tree
And the splashing of rain.
Only the sand we know
And the cloudless sky,
The mirage and the deep-sunk well
And the stars on high.

To the sound of our bells we came
With huge soft stride,
Kings riding upon our backs,
Slaves at our side,
Out of the East drawn on
By a dream and a star,
Seeking the hills and the groves
Where the fixed towns are.

Our goal was no palace gate,
No temple of old,
But a child in his mother's lap,
In the cloudy cold.
The olives were windy and white,
Dust swirled through the town,
As all in their royal robes
Our masters knelt down.

Then back to the desert we paced
In our phantom state,
And faded again in the sands
That are secret as fate—
Portents of glory and danger
Our dark shadows lay
At the feet of the babe in the manger,
And then drifted away.

Elizabeth Coatsworth, 20th century

Merry Christmas

I saw on the snow
when I tried my skis
the track of a mouse
beside some trees.

Before he tunneled
to reach his house
he wrote "Merry Christmas"
in white, in mouse.

Aileen Fisher, 20th century

Carol

Villagers all, this frosty tide,
Let your door swing open wide,
Though wind may follow, and snow beside,
Yet draw us in by your fire to bide;
    Joy shall be yours in the morning!

Here we stand in the cold and the sleet,
Blowing fingers and stamping feet,
Come from far away you to greet—
You by the fire and we in the street—
    Bidding you joy in the morning!

For ere one half of the night was gone,
Sudden a star has led us on,
Raining bliss and benison—
Bliss tomorrow and more anon,
    Joy for every morning!

Goodman Joseph toiled through the snow—
Saw the star o'er a stable low;
Mary she might no farther go—
Welcome thatch, and little below!
    Joy was hers in the morning!

And then they heard the angels tell
"Who were the first to cry Nowell?
Animals all, as it befell,
In the stable where they did dwell!
Joy shall be theirs in the morning!

Kenneth Grahame, 1859–1932

❦ *Wood's Litany*

Now birds that sleep in brittle trees,
Sparrows and jays and chickadees,
The last, last robin and the crow,
Awake beneath your thatch of snow
And hearing bells of midnight ring
Rouse up and through the darkness sing
How in your dreams across the snows
A star, bright as a sun, arose.

And all you creatures furred and wise
That in the darkness close bright eyes,
Twitch quivering nostrils, leave your sleep
And from your dens and hollows creep.
See how the deer among the thorns
Raises the crosses of his horns,
While like soft candles at a feast
The doe's eyes turn to face the east!

Gentle is he
As windless snow.
Kind as a tree
With shelter below.

As a stream of water
In August heat,
As a blueberry bush
Hidden and sweet,

Such is he
Who is born this day
In Bethlehem
So far away!

Elizabeth Coatsworth, 20th century

❦ *The Friendly Beasts*

Jesus our brother, strong and good,
Was humbly born in a stable rude,
And the friendly beasts around Him stood,
Jesus our brother, strong and good.

"I," said the donkey, shaggy and brown,
"I carried His mother uphill and down,
I carried her safely to Bethlehem town;
I," said the donkey shaggy and brown.

"I," said the cow, all white and red,
"I gave Him my manger for His bed,
I gave Him my hay to pillow His head,
I," said the cow all white and red.

"I," said the sheep with curly horn,
"I gave Him my wool for His blanket warm,
He wore my coat on Christmas morn;
I," said the sheep with curly horn.

"I," said the dove, from the rafters high,
"Cooed Him to sleep, my mate and I;
We cooed Him to sleep, my mate and I;
I," said the dove, from the rafters high.

And every beast by some good spell,
In the stable dark was glad to tell,
Of the gift he gave Immanuel,
The gift he gave Immanuel.

English carol, 12th century

I Heard a Bird Sing

I Heard a Bird Sing

I heard a bird sing
   In the dark of December,
A magical thing
   And sweet to remember

We are nearer to spring
   Than we were in September,
I heard a bird sing
   In the dark of December

Oliver Herford, 1863–1935

From gable, barn, and stable
Protrudes the birdies' table
Spread with a sheaf of corn.

Old Norwegian verse

☙ *The Stork*
A Christmas Ballad

The stork she rose on Christmas Eve
And said unto her brood,
"I now must fare to Bethlehem
To view the Son of God."

She gave to each his dole of meat,
She stowed them fairly in,
And fair she flew and fast she flew
And came to Bethlehem.

"Now where is he of David's line?"
She asked at house and hall.
"He is not here at all," they said
"But in the manger stall."

She found him in the manger stall
With that most holy maid;
The gentle stork she wept to see
The Lord so rudely laid.

Then from her panting breast she plucked
The feathers white and warm;
She strewed them in the manger bed
To keep the Lord from harm.

"Now blessed be the gentle stork
Forever more," quoth He,
"Because she saw my sorry state
And showed pity."

Full welcome shall she ever be
In hamlet and in hall,
And named henceforth the Blessed Bird
And friend of babies all."

from the fly-leaf of King Edward's Prayer Book, *1549* (*with modern spelling*)

Carol of the Birds

Whence comes this rush of wings afar,
Following straight the Noël star?
Birds from the woods in wondrous flight,
Bethlehem seek this Holy Night.

"Tell us, ye birds, why come ye here,
Into this stable, poor and drear?"
"Hast'ning we seek the new-born King,
And all our sweetest music bring."

Hark how the green-finch bears his part,
Philomel, too, with tender heart,
Chants from her leafy dark retreat,
Re, mi, fa, sol, in accents sweet.

Angels and shepherds, birds of the sky,
Come where the Son of God doth lie;
Christ on earth with man doth dwell,
Join in the shout, Noël, Noël.

an old French carol from Bas Quercy

Carol of the Birds

A star rose in the sky
and glory from on high
did fill the night with splendor.
Came birds with joyful voice
to carol and rejoice with
songs so sweet and tender.
Came birds with joyful voice
to carol and rejoice with
songs so sweet and tender.

The eagle then did rise,
went flying through the skies,
to tell the wondrous story,
sang, Jesus, born is he,
from sin we are set free,
he brings us joy and glory.

The sparrow with delight
said, This is Christmas night,
our happiness revealing.
The sky with praises rang,
as finch and robin sang—
oh, what a happy feeling!

The lark upon the wing
said, Now it seems like spring,
no more is winter pressing;
for now a flower is born
whose fragrance on this morn
to earth brings heaven's blessing.

Sang magpie, thrush, and jay,
It seems the month of May
in answer to our yearning.
The trees again are green
and blossoms now are seen,
it is the spring returning!

The cuckoo sang, Come, come,
And celebrate the dawn
this glorious aurora.
The raven from his throat
then trilled a festive note
to the unexcelled Señora.

The partridge then confessed,
I want to build my nest
beneath that very gable
where I may see the Child
and watch whene'er he smiles
with Mary in that stable.

Old Spanish carol from Catalonia

Eerily Sweet

The cocks are crowing
To the stars,
One crows to Venus,
And one to Mars.

Like trumpets blown
Across the snow
Eerily sweet
The proud cocks crow.

"It is not dawn
O birds of the sun!
On the Milky Way
Still flies the Swan,

"And great Orion
Strides through the air,
And Berenice
Lets down her hair.

"It is not dawn
O birds of the day!
Why do you crow
With the sun far away?"

The cocks crow loud
And the cocks crow clear,
Across the snow
'Tis a joy to hear.

"Once long ago
When the world was young
Over a manger
A bright star hung.

"Marvelled both man
And beast at the sight,
But the cocks saluted
The holy light.

"Proudly they stood
And clapped their wings
To welcome the star
Of the King of kings!

"And now sometimes
Across the snow
We remember that night
And rise, and crow,

"And repeat the chant
To that star thrice blest—
'Christus, Christus
Natus est!' "

Like trumpets blown
Across the snow
Eerily sweet
The proud cocks crow.

Elizabeth Coatsworth, 20th century

The Brown Birds

Scant is the holly,
The holly-berries few!
There's a bunch for the rich man
To see his Christmas through,
And a spray or a sprig
For the pretty-well-to-do,
But what of the brown birds
Whom hunger maketh bold?
What of the poor birds
A-seeking in the cold?
Oh, when the holly's scant
And the holly-berries few,
What will the brown birds,
The poor birds do?

Eleanor Farjeon, 1881–1965

The Three Kings

❦ *The Magi*

When they had heard the king, they departed; and, lo, the star, which they saw in the east, went before them, till it came and stood over where the young child was.

When they saw the star, they rejoiced with exceeding great joy.

And when they were come into the house, they saw the young child with Mary his mother, and fell down, and worshipped him: and when they had opened their treasures, they presented unto him gifts; gold, and frankincense, and myrrh.

Matthew II:9–11

❦ *Three Kings*

Three kings came out of Indian land
    To see the wondrous Infant bent,
With splendid presents in their hand;
    Straightly a star before them went.
A wondrous thing it was to see:
    That star was more than other three.

Old English Epiphany carol

❦ *The Three Kings*

"I am Gaspar. I have brought frankincense,
and I have come here to say that life is good.
That God exists. That love is everything.
I know it is so because of the heavenly star."

"I am Melchior. I have brought fragrant myrrh.
Yes, God exists. He is the light of day.
The white flower is rooted in the mud,
and all delights are tinged with melancholy."

"I am Balthasar. I have brought gold.
I assure you, God exists. He is great and strong.
I know it is so because of the perfect star
that shines so brightly in Death's diadem."

"Gaspar, Melchior, Balthasar: be still.
Love has triumphed, and bids you to its feast.
Christ, reborn, turns chaos into light,
and on His brow He wears the Crown of Life."

Rubén Darío, 1867–1916,
translated by Lysander Kemp

❦ *The Kings from the East*

"Dear children," they asked in every town,
  Three kings from the land of the sun,
"Which is the road to Bethlehem?"
  But neither the old nor the young

Could tell, so the kings rode on:
  Their guide was a golden star,
Which glittered ahead of them, high in the air,
  So clear, so very clear.

The star stood still over Joseph's house,
  They all of them stepped in:
The good ox lowed and the little child cried,
And the kings began to sing.

Heinrich Heine, 1797–1856

❦ *Carol of the Brown King*

Of the three Wise Men
Who came to the King,
One was a brown man,
So they sing.

Of the three Wise Men
Who followed the Star,
One was a brown king
From afar.

They brought fine gifts
Of spices and gold
In jeweled boxes
Of beauty untold.

Unto His humble
Manger they came
And bowed their heads
In Jesus' name.

Three Wise Men,
One dark like me—
Part of His
Nativity.

Langston Hughes, 20th century

Farewell to Christmas

Noel is leaving us,
Sad it is to tell,
But he will come again,
Adieu, Noel.

His wife and his children
Weep as they go.
On a gray horse,
They ride through the snow.

The kings ride away
In the snow and the rain,
After twelve months,
We shall see them again.

French Epiphany carol

Flood with Light
Earth's Darkest Places

❦ *Winter Solstice Chant*

Our half of the earth has tipped away from you
and we are on the winter side of the sun.
When we are in cold and darkness,
We see you in candles and fires.
We have stored your energy to feed us
Until the time you warm us thru our skin.

from Being of the Sun
by Ramon Sender and Alice Bay Laurel

Sing, ye heavens, tell the story,
Of his glory,
Till his praises
Flood with light earth's darkest places!

Philipp Nicolai, 19th century

"Look!" The Earth is aflame with
delight
O sons of the morning rejoice at the
sight.
Everywhere, everywhere Christmas
tonight.

from A Christmas Carol
by Phillips Brooks, 1835–1893

But Peaceful Was the Night

But peaceful was the night
Wherein the Prince of Light
His reign of peace upon the earth began:
The winds with wonder whist,
Smoothly the waters kissed,
Whispering new joys to the mild Ocean,
Who now hath quite forgot to rave,
While birds of calm sit brooding on the charmed
wave.

from On the Morning of Christ's Nativity
by John Milton, 1608–1674

During the Christmas season in
old Russia, people sang Kolyada
songs. An ancient word, Kolyada
may refer to the sun or a wheel.
When Christmas came to Russia,
the Kolyada songs became part of it.

"Kolyada" "Kolyada"
Kolyada has arrived,
On the Eve of the Nativity,
Holy Kolyada,
Through all the courts, in all the alleys.
We found Kolyada
In Peter's Court.
Round Peter's Court there is an iron fence,
In the midst of the court there are three
rooms,
In the first room is the bright Moon,
In the second room the red Sun,
And in the third room, the many stars.

Russian carol

I Sing the Birth

I sing the birth was born to-night,
The Author both of life and light;
    The angels so did sound it.
And like the ravish'd shepherds said,
Who saw the light, and were afraid,
    Yet search'd, and true they found it.

Ben Jonson, 1573–1637

You Light

Vertical light,
light you;
You high light,
gold light;
vibrant light,
light you.
And I the black, blind, deaf, mute, horizontal
    shadow.

Juan Ramón Jiménez, 1881–1958

Dimmest and brightest month am I;
My short days end, my lengthening days begin;
What matters more or less sun in the sky,
When all is sun within?

Christina Georgina Rossetti, 1830–1894

Our Joyful'st Feast

❦ *Christmas Tree*

I'll find me a spruce
in the cold white wood
with wide green boughs
and a snowy hood.

I'll pin on a star
with five gold spurs
to mark my spruce
from the pines and firs.

I'll make me a score
of suet balls
to tie to my spruce
when the cold dusk falls,

And I'll hear next day
from the sheltering trees,
the Christmas carols
of the chickadees.

Aileen Fisher, 20th century

❧ *Christmas Goes to Sea*

I saw a fishing boat steer by,
Blunt-prowed beneath the winter sky,
As Christmas dusk was falling.

The hull was crusted dark with spray,
The waters all about spread gray,
And sea gulls followed calling.

But to the masthead gallantly
Was lashed a little Christmas tree,
A green-armed pledge of pine.

No bright festoons or gifts it bore,
And yet those empty boughs held more
Than tinsel for a sign.

So fair a sight it was to see—
That small, seafaring Christmas tree
High amid shroud and spar.

And all night long I thought of it
Salt-drenched, wind-buffeted, and lit
By Bethlehem's bright star.

Rachel Field, 20th century

❧ *Yolka*

What merriment, what merriment,
We're here in happy throng.
We greet you, Yolka, gleefully
With season's gayest song.

from Yolka *by Marguerita Rudolph*

Note: A *yolka* is a little fir tree in Russian.

❧ *City Lights*

Into the endless dark
The lights of the buildings shine,
Row upon twinkling row,
Line upon glistening line.
Up and up they mount
Till the tallest seems to be
The topmost taper set
On a towering Christmas tree.

Rachel Field, 20th century

The Mahogany Tree

Christmas is here;
Winds whistle shrill,
Icy and chill,
Little care we:
Little we fear
Weather without,
Sheltered about
The Mahogany Tree.

Commoner greens,
Ivy and oaks,
Poets, in jokes,
Sing, do you see?
Good fellows' shins
Here, boys, are found,
Twisting around
The Mahogany Tree.

Once on the boughs
Birds of rare plume
Sang, in its bloom;
Night birds are we:
Here we carouse,
Singing like them,
Perched round the stem
Of the jolly old tree.

Here let us sport,
Boys, as we sit;
Laughter and wit
Flashing so free.

Sorrows, begone!
Life and its ills,
Duns and their bills,
Bid we to flee.

Life is but short—
When we are gone,
Let them sing on,
Round the old tree.

Evenings we knew,
Happy as this;
Faces we miss,
Pleasant to see.
Kind hearts and true,
Gentle and just,
Peace to your dust!
We sing round the tree.

Care, like a dun,
Lurks at the gate:
Let the dog wait;
Happy we'll be!
Drink every one;
Pile up the coals,
Fill the red bowls,
Round the old tree.

Drain we the cup.—
Friend, art afraid?
Spirits are laid
In the Red Sea.
Mantle it up;
Empty it yet;
Let us forget,
Round the old tree.

Come with the dawn,
Blue-devil sprite;
Leave us to-night,
Round the old tree.

William Makepeace Thackeray, 1811–1863

❦ *The Tree*

Now in white
Winter of snowing
We get our tree:
Green hue of growing.

It comes to stay
With us inside,
To be green life
In its green pride.

Now at the sleepy
End of year,
It lives with us
For our green cheer.

Paul Engle, 20th century

I'll Find Me a Spruce

O you merry, merry souls,
  Christmas is a-coming;
We shall have flowing bowls,
  Dancing, piping, drumming.

Delicate minced pies,
  To feast every maiden,
Capon and goose likewise,
  Brawn, and dish of sturgeon.

Then for your Christmas-box
  Sweet plum-cakes and money,
Delicate Holland smocks,
  Kisses sweet as honey.

Hey for the Christmas ball,
  Where we shall be jolly;
Coupling short and tall,
  Kate, Dick, Ralph, and Molly.

from Round About Our Coal Fire, *1734*

Dame, get up and bake your pies,
Bake your pies, bake your pies,
Dame, get up and bake your pies,
On Christmas Day in the morning.

English traditional

The Christmas Pudding

Into the basin put the plums,
Stirabout, stirabout, stirabout!

Next the good white flour comes,
Stirabout, stirabout, stirabout!

Sugar and peel and eggs and spice,
Stirabout, stirabout, stirabout!

Mix them and fix them and cook them twice,
Stirabout, stirabout, stirabout!

English traditional

Flower of England, fruit of Spain,
Met together in a shower of rain,
Put in a bag and tied with a string,
If you guess the answer, I'll give you a pin.

English riddle

[Answer: A Christmas pudding]

❦ *Our Joyful'st Feast*

Lo, now is come our joyful'st feast!
  Let every man be jolly,
Each room with ivy leaves is dressed,
  And every post with holly.
Now all our neighbors' chimneys smoke,
  And Christmas blocks are burning;
Their ovens they with baked meats choke
  And all their spits are turning.
    Without the door let sorrow lie,
    And if, for cold, it hap to die,
    We'll bury it in a Christmas pie,
    And evermore be merry.

George Wither, 1588–1667

"Now that the time has come wherein
  Our Saviour Christ was born,
The larder's full of beef and pork,
  The garner's full of corn;
As God hath plenty to thee sent,
  Take comfort of thy labors,
And let it never thee repent
  To feast thy needy neighbors."

from Poor Robin's Almanack, *1700*

❦ *Now Thrice Welcome Christmas*

Now thrice welcome Christmas,
    Which brings us good-cheer,
Minced pies and plum-porridge,
    Good ale and strong beer;
With pig, goose, and capon,
    The best that can be,
So well doth the weather
    And our stomachs agree.

Observe how the chimneys
    Do smoke all about,
The cooks are providing
    For dinner no doubt.

from Poor Robin's Almanack, *1695*

Yule, yule, yule, my belly's full
Cracking nuts and crying yule, yule, yule!

English traditional

Old Christmas Returned

All you that to feasting and mirth are inclined,
Come here is good news for to pleasure your
mind,
Old Christmas is come for to keep open house,
He scorns to be guilty of starving a mouse:
Then come, boys, and welcome for diet the
chief,
Plum-pudding, goose, capon, minced pies, and
roast beef.

The holly and ivy about the walls wind
And show that we ought to our neighbors be
kind,
Inviting each other for pastime and sport,
And where we best fare, there we most do
resort;
We fail not of victuals, and that of the chief,
Plum-pudding, goose, capon, minced pies, and
roast beef.

All travellers, as they do pass on their way,
At gentlemen's halls are invited to stay,
Themselves to refresh, and their horses to rest,
Since that he must be Old Christmas's guest;
Nay, the poor shall not want, but have for relief,
Plum-pudding, goose, capon, minced pies, and
roast beef.

Old English carol

❦ *Stop Thief!*

Come, guard this night the Christmas-pie,
That the thief, though ne'er so sly,
With his flesh-hooks, don't come nigh
To catch it

From him who all alone sits there,
Having his eyes still in his ear,
And a deal of nightly fear,
To watch it.

Robert Herrick, 1591–1674

❦ *Duckle, Duckle, Daisy*

Duckle, duckle, daisy
Martha must be crazy,
She went and made a Christmas cake
Of olive oil and gluten-flake,
And put it in the sink to bake,
Duckle, duckle, daisy.

Leroy F. Jackson, 20th century

Now Christmas is come
Let's beat up the drum,
And call all our neighbors together,
And when they appear,
Let's make them such cheer
As will keep out the wind and the weather.

from The Sketch Book *by*
Washington Irving, 1783–1859

Draw Round the Fire

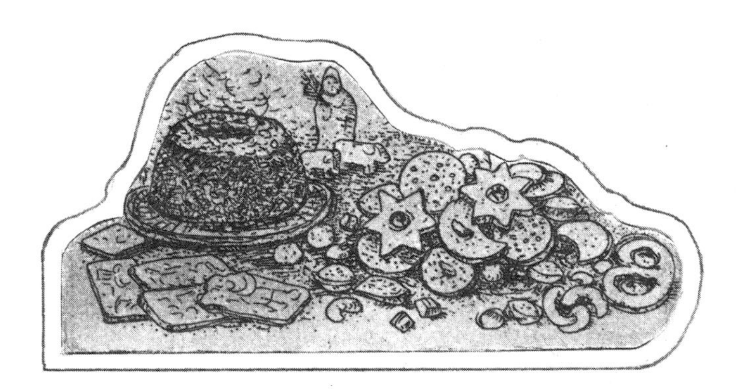

Feed the wood and have a
joyful minute,
For the seeds of earthly suns
are in it.

Johann Wolfgang von Goethe, 1749–1832

The Yule Log

Come bring with a noise,
My merry, merry boys,
The Christmas log to the firing;
While my good dame, she
Bids ye all be free,
And drink to your heart's desiring.

With the last year's brand
Light the new block, and
For good success in his spending,
On your psalteries play,
That sweet luck may
Come while the log is a tending.

Robert Herrick, 1591–1674

Now blocks to cleave
This time requires,
'Gainst Christmas for
To make good fires.

from Poor Robin's Almanack, *1677*

Heap on more wood—the wind is chill;
But let it whistle as it will,
We'll keep our Christmas merry still.

from Marmion, *by*
Sir Walter Scott, 1771–1832

❦*A Catch by the Hearth*

Sing we all merrily
    Christmas is here,
The day that we love best
    Of days in the year.

Bring forth the holly,
    The box, and the bay.
Deck out our cottage
    For glad Christmas Day.

Sing we all merrily,
    Draw round the fire,
Sister and brother,
    Grandson and sire.

Author unknown

Welcome, Dear St. Nicholas, Santa Claus, and Father Christmas

❦ *When Santa Claus Comes*

A good time is coming, I wish it were here,
The very best time in the whole of the year;
I'm counting each day on my fingers and
thumbs—
The weeks that must pass before Santa Claus
comes.

Then when the first snowflakes begin to come
down,
And the wind whistles sharp and the branches
are brown,
I'll not mind the cold, though my fingers it
numbs,
For it brings the time nearer when Santa Claus
comes.

Author unknown

The Ballad of Befana
An Epiphany Legend

Befana the Housewife, scrubbing her pane,
Saw three old sages ride down the lane,
Saw three gray travelers pass her door—
Gaspar, Balthazar, Melchior.

"Where journey you, sirs?" she asked of them.
Balthazar answered, "To Bethlehem,
For we have news of a marvelous thing.
Born in a stable is Christ the King."

"Give Him my welcome!"
Then Gaspar smiled,
"Come with us, mistress, to greet the Child."

"Oh, happily, happily would I fare,
Were my dusting through and I'd polished the
stair."

Old Melchior leaned on his saddle horn,
"Then send but a gift to the small Newborn."

"Oh, gladly, gladly, I'd send Him one,
Were the hearthstone swept and my weaving
done.

"As soon as ever I've baked my bread,
I'll fetch Him a pillow for His head,
And a coverlet, too," Befana said.

"When the rooms are aired and the linen dry,
I'll look at the Babe."
But the Three rode by.

She worked for a day and a night and a day,
Then gifts in her hands, took up her way.
But she never could find where the Christ Child
lay.

And still she wanders at Christmastide,
Houseless, whose house was all her pride,

Whose heart was tardy, whose gifts were late;
Wanders, and knocks at every gate,
Crying, "Good people, the bells begin!
Put off your toiling and let love in."

Phyllis McGinley, 20th century

Saint Nicholas, my dear good friend
To serve you ever was my end,
If you will, me something give,
I'll serve you ever while I live.

Author unknown

❦ *Old Santa Is an Active Man*

Old Santa is an active man,
    He slides down chimneys black,
Fills stockings while his reindeer wait,
    And then goes dashing back!

Lois Lenski, 20th century

❦*Granny Winter*

Snow has carpeted the ground;
It's the season's best.
Snowflakes falling all around
Our welcome Guest!

Granny Winter's come with Yolka
Cheerily she sings.
Bags of sweets and treats and trinkets
Every year she brings.

Dressed in white and full of sparkles,
Smiling, bright and gay;
Granny Winter's coming, speeding,
Singing all the way:

"For your fun and for your pleasure,
Darling girls and boys,
I've brought spinning tops and wagons,
Dolls and other toys.

"But, to any mischief-maker,
This is what I'll say:
'I can't give you any presents,
Not this holiday.' "

Remembered from childhood and adapted from the Russian by Marguerita Rudolph, 20th century

Old Saint Nicholas comes so speedily
Over the frozen snow,
Lots of eatables, lots of drinkables,
Coming for me, I know . . .

from Germany, author unknown

Santa Claus

He comes in the night! He comes in the night!
He softly, silently comes,
While the little brown heads on the pillows so white
Are dreaming of bugles and drums.
He cuts thro' the snow like a ship thro' the foam,
While the white flakes 'round him whirl.
Who tells him I know not, but he findeth the home
Of each good little boy and girl.

His sleigh it is long, and deep, and wide;
  It will carry a host of things,
While dozens of drums hang over the side,
  With the sticks sticking under the strings.
And yet not the sound of a drum is heard,
  Not a bugle blast is blown,
As he mounts to the chimney-top like a bird,
  And drops to the hearth like a stone.

The little red stockings he silently fills,
  Till the stockings will hold no more;
The bright little sleds for the great snow hills
  Are quickly set down on the floor.
Then Santa Claus mounts to the roof like a bird,
  And glides to his seat in the sleigh;
Not the sound of a bugle or drum is heard
  As he noiselessly gallops away.

Anonymous, 1880

❦*A Christmas Eve Thought*

If Santa Claus should stumble,
As he climbs the chimney tall
With all this ice upon it,
I'm afraid he'd get a fall
And smash himself to pieces—
To say nothing of the toys!
Dear me, what sorrow that would bring
To all the girls and boys!
So I am going to write a note
And pin it to the gate,—
I'll write it large, so he can see,
No matter if it's late,—
And say, "Dear Santa Claus, don't try
To climb the roof to-night,
But walk right in, the door's unlocked,
The nursery's on the right!"

Harriet Brewer Sterling
St. Nicholas, *December, 1895*

Conversation Between Mr. and Mrs. Santa Claus

(Overheard at the North Pole Early
Christmas Morning)

"Are the reindeer in the rain, dear?"
Asked Mrs. Santa Claus.
"No. I put them in the barn, dear,
To dry their little paws."

"Is the sleigh, sir, put away, sir,
In the barn beside the deer?"
"Yes, I'm going to get it ready
To use again next year."

"And the pack, dear, is it back, dear?"
"Yes. It's empty of its toys,
And tomorrow I'll start filling it,
For next year's girls and boys."

Rowena Bennett, 20th century

Do Not Open Until Christmas

❦ *Do Not Open Until Christmas*

I shake-shake,
Shake-shake,
Shake the package well.

But what there is
Inside of it,
Shaking will not tell.

James S. Tippett, 20th century

❦ *Bundles*

A bundle is a funny thing,
It always sets me wondering;
For whether it is thin or wide
You never know just what's inside.

Especially on Christmas week,
Temptation is so great to peek!
Now wouldn't it be much more fun
If shoppers carried things undone?

John Farrar, 20th century

Stocking Song on Christmas Eve

Welcome, Christmas! heel and toe
Here we wait thcc in a row.
Come, good Santa Claus, we beg,—
Fill us tightly, foot and leg.

Fill us quickly ere you go,—
Fill us till we overflow.
That's the way! and leave us more
Heaped in piles upon the floor.

Little feet that ran all day
Twitch in dreams of merry play;
Little feet that jumped at will
Lie all pink, and warm, and still.

See us, how we lightly swing;
Hear us, how we try to sing.
Welcome, Christmas! heel and toe,
Come and fill us ere you go.

Here we hang till some one nimbly
Jumps with treasure down the chimney.
Bless us! how he'll tickle us!
Funny old St. Nicholas!

Mary Mapes Dodge, 1831–1905

❦ *A Christmas Carol*

In the bleak mid-winter
  Frosty wind made moan,
Earth stood hard as iron,
  Water like a stone;
Snow had fallen, snow on snow,
  Snow on snow,
In the bleak mid-winter
  Long ago.

Our God, Heaven cannot hold him
  Nor earth sustain;
Heaven and earth shall flee away
  When he comes to reign:
In the bleak mid-winter
  A stable-place sufficed
The Lord God Almighty
  Jesus Christ.

Enough for him, whom cherubim
  Worship night and day,
A breastful of milk
  And a mangerful of hay;
Enough for him, whom angels
  Fall down before,
The ox and ass and camel
  Which adore.

Angels and archangels
  May have gathered there,
Cherubim and seraphim
  Thronged the air;
But only his mother
  In her maiden bliss
Worshipped the Beloved
  With a kiss.

What can I give him,
  Poor as I am?
If I were a shepherd
  I would bring a lamb,
If I were a Wise Man
  I would do my part,—
Yet what I can I give him,
  Give my heart.

Christina Georgina Rossetti, 1830–1894

Oh, Christmas time is drawing near,
  And then I shall have money;
I'll save it up, and, box and all,
  I'll give it to my honey.

from an 18th century ballad

❦ *An Anonymous Verse from a Puerto Rican Christmas card*

Lady Santa Ana
Why does the Child cry?

About an orange He's lost
and cannot spy.

Tell Him not to cry
For I have two—

One for the Child
And one for you.

Translated from the Spanish
by Langston Hughes, 20th century

❦ *Gift*

Christmas morning I
got up before the others and
ran
naked across the plank
floor into the front
room to see grandma
sewing a new
button on my last year's
ragdoll.

Carol Freeman, 20th century

❦ *Country Christmas*

Let's hang up some suet
for juncos and jays,
let's put out some hay for the deer,
let's throw in some corn
where the cottontail stays,
this holiday season of year.

Let's scatter some millet
and barley and wheat—
it isn't much trouble or fuss
to give all the wild folk
a holiday treat
so they can have Christmas, like us!

Aileen Fisher, 20th century

To Wish You a Merry Christmas

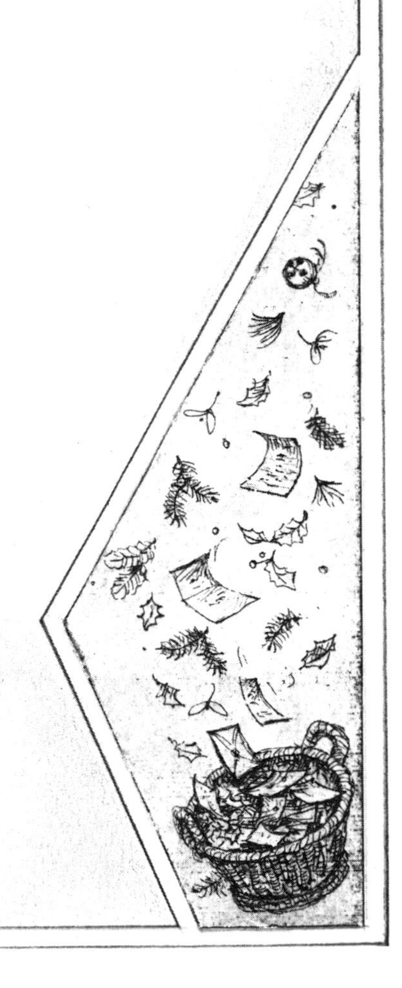

At Christmas, play and make good cheer,
For Christmas comes but once a year.

Thomas Tusser, 1524–1580

Christmas Wish

May your tree
this Christmas
be a pine tree,
spicy-fragrant,
full-needled,
to bring you
new knowledge
of immortality.
May there be
pine cones
on your tree—
abundance
of life.
And nestled
in the branches
may there be
a bird's nest,
old old symbol
of happiness.

Elizabeth Searle Lamb, 20th century

M for the Music, merry and clear;
E for the Eve, the crown of the year;
R for the Romping of bright girls and boys;
R for the Reindeer that bring them the toys;
Y for the Yule-log softly aglow.

C for the Cold of the sky and the snow;
H for the Hearth where they hang up the hose;
R for the Reel which the old folks propose;
I for the Icicles seen through the pane;
S for the Sleigh-bells, with tinkling refrain;
T for the Tree with gifts all a-bloom
M for the Mistletoe hung in the room;
A for the Anthems we all love to hear;
S for ST. Nicholas—joy of the year!

from St. Nicholas, *January, 1897*

He comes—the brave old Christmas!
    His sturdy steps I hear;
We will give him a hearty welcome,
    For he comes but once a year!

English, 19th century

    Man, be merry
    As birds on berry,
And all thy care let away.

Author unknown

May God bless your Christmas;
May it last until Easter.

Scandinavian

Sing hey! Sing hey!
For Christmas Day;
Twine mistletoe and holly,
For friendship flows
In winter snows,
And so let's all be jolly.

English traditional

May each be found thus as the year circles
round,
With mirth and good humor each Christmas be
crowned,
And may all who have plenty of riches in store
With their bountiful blessings make happy the
poor;
For never as yet it was counted a crime,
To be merry and cheery at that happy time.

from an 18th century broadside

Bounce buckram, velvets dear,
Christmas comes but once a year,
When it comes it brings good cheer,
And when it's gone it's never near.

English traditional

Christmas Pies

Without the door let sorrow lie,
And if for cold it hap to die,
We'll bury it in Christmas pie,
  And evermore be merry!

English traditional

Rejoice and be glad
Open your bag
And fill our handkerchiefs
Hallelujah! Hallelujah!

Armenian traditional

Yule, yule, yule,
Three puddings in a pulc,
Crack nuts and cry yule!

Old nonsense rhyme

Welcome be ye that are here,
Welcome all, and make good cheer;
Welcome all another year
        Welcome Yule!

English, 15th century

Welcome be Thou, heavenly King,
Welcome born on this morning,
Welcome, for whom we shall sing
        Welcome Yule!

English, 15th century

I wish you a merry Christmas
And a happy New Year;
A pocket full of money
And a cellar full of beer,
And a great fat pig
To last you all the year.

English traditional

God bless the master of this house
  Likewise the mistress too.
May their barns be filled with wheat and corn,
  And their hearts be always true.

A merry Christmas is our wish
  Where'er we do appear,
To you a well-filled purse, a well-filled dish,
  And a happy bright New Year!

English wassailers' song

Yule's Come and Yule's Gone

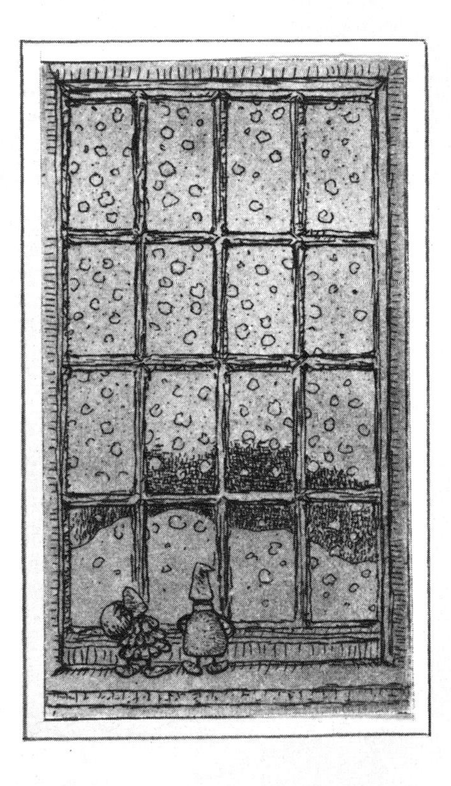

❦ *Now Have Good Day*

Now have good day, now have good day.
I am Christmas, and now I go my way.

Here have I dwelt with more or less,
From Hallow-tide till Candlemas,
And now must I from you hence pass,
          Now have good day.

English traditional, c. 1540

Yule's come and yule's gone,
And we have feasted well,
So Jock must to his flail again
And Jenny to her wheel.

Scottish traditional

❦ *Spring Cleaning*

Down with the rosemary and bays,
    Down with the mistletoe;
Instead of holly, now up-raise
    The greener box, for show.

The holly hitherto did sway;
    Let box now domineer,
Until the dancing Easter-day,
    On Easter's Eve appear.

Robert Herrick, 1591–1674

Superstitions and Sayings

❦ *People Once Believed That . . .*

- on Christmas Eve, angels passed over all springs, making the water pure.

- it was good luck for the first person up on Christmas Day to open a door and "let Christmas in."

- a candle left burning all night in an empty room on Christmas Eve would bring light, warmth, and plenty all year.

- if a Christmas candle went out or was blown out before morning, that was a bad omen.

- if you smeared the plough with the stub of your Yule candle at the first spring plowing, it would ensure good crops.

- stubs of Yule candles burned during a thunderstorm would protect the house from lightning.

- bells and chimes should be sounded on Christmas Day to frighten away evil spirits.

- church bells destroyed or broken on Christmas Day would ring every December 25th from then on.

- if Christmas bells tolled on a Saturday, the winter would be foggy and the summer cold.

- bells placed near a baby or small child would keep evil spirits away.

- holly placed in windows would protect a home from evil.

- to let mistletoe fall to the ground was unlucky.

- a sprig of mistletoe hung over a stable door would keep the cattle healthy.

- holly planted near a house would frighten off witches and protect the dwelling from thunder and lightning.

- a sprig of holly on the bedpost brought happy dreams.

- anyone who was not kissed under the mistletoe would not marry during the following year.

- cows who bore calves during the Christmas holidays should be fed mistletoe to keep themselves and their young healthy.

- those who failed to take down all evergreens and destroy them by Twelfth Night would be haunted by evil spirits.

- it was unlucky to turn anyone away on Christmas Eve. The stranger at the door might be the Christ Child in disguise.

- a sick baby should be taken to the door on Christmas Eve. If it recovered, this meant that the Christ Child had touched it. If it died, this meant that the Christ Child needed a playmate in Heaven.

- a person born on Christmas Day would have the power to see and command spirits, and to predict the future.

- a child born on Christmas Day would be "fair and wise and good."

- on Christmas Eve, sheep walked in procession.

- bees hummed Christmas Carols.

- roosters crowed all night.

- farm animals knelt in their stalls on Christmas Eve, and, for one hour, all animals could speak.

- a cricket chirping at Christmas time brought good luck.

- a girl might knock on the gate to the pigsty on Christmas Eve. If a full-grown hog was the first to grunt in reply, her husband would be an old man. If a piglet replied, he would be a young man.

- farm animals might gossip about the faults of anyone who listened in on their conversations on Christmas Eve.

- sheep, cattle, and horses compared notes on how they had been treated during the past year.

- a person born between eleven and twelve o'clock on Christmas Eve could understand what the animals said.

- if a cat meowed on Christmas Eve, bad luck would follow. Therefore every house cat should be given all it could eat on Christmas Eve.

- cows should be treated kindly because cattle at Bethlehem breathed upon the Christ Child to keep Him warm.

- sparks from a Yule Log would create warmth in human souls.

- it was unlucky to light the Yule log before Christmas.

- ashes from a Yule log could cure many diseases.

- the number of sparks from a Yule log showed the number of farm animals that would be born during the coming year.

- while the Yule log was burning, it was bad luck to have a barefooted or flat-footed person in the room.

- if the person tending the Yule fire had dirty hands, the fire wouldn't burn well.

- part of the Yule log must be kept to start the Christmas fire the next year.

- bread baked on Christmas Eve would never become moldy.

- if a girl ate a cake made of flour, water, and salt on Christmas Eve, she would dream of her future husband.

- lentils soaked and planted in a bowl would rekindle life in sick people who had given up hope.

- the number of days between the first snowfall and Christmas told how many snowfalls would come before spring.

- a fruit tree could be made to bear by tying a band of straw around the trunk or by beating it with a whip on Christmas Day.

- if the sun shone through the fruit trees at noon on Christmas Day, there would be a good crop.

- after Christmas came Lent, after feasting, fasting.

- a green Christmas meant a white Easter.

- snow on Christmas meant that Easter would be green.

Index of Authors, Titles, and First Lines

Authors' names and first lines of poems are in upper and lower case Roman. Titles of poems appear in italics.